Where Have the Dragons Gone?

I hope you enjoy the book! To Cody Bryan 7/5/2003

WRITTEN BY BRYAN AUXIER
ILLUSTRATED BY REGINA DANIELS
PUBLISHED BY WHERE? PRESS, INC.
Paintsville, KY
©2002

Where? Press, Inc.

Dedicated to the memory of my dad, ***Ray Auxier***,
who died from lung cancer on January 5, 1998.
We will always love you! - BRYAN

Long ago dragons lived all throughout the land of Britain. For a time the dragons were as free as any other creature on Earth. However during the time of the Great King, dragons were being hunted and killed by his knights. This frightened the dragons very much. They feared that if they didn't do something, they would all soon be gone.

There were four types of dragons: Emerald, Crimson, Golden, and Komodo. There was also a Grand Dragon who served as their leader. The clan leaders along with the Grand Dragon formed the dragon council called the Kruppa.

Brenthos, the Grand Dragon, called a special meeting. "I have called us together to discuss our problem with the king and his knights. I would like to hear suggestions from each of you on how best to solve it."

Beryl, the Emerald leader, addressed the council first. "Most powerful Brenthos and Kruppa members, I say we join our clans together in battle and attack the knights on four sides. After we have burned the castle and killed the king and his knights, we can destroy the remaining humans and have the earth to ourselves as it should be."

"Your suggestion will be considered," remarked Brenthos.

Carmine from the Crimson Clan spoke before the Kruppa next. "Honorable Brenthos and Kruppa, I believe we should try to establish peace between ourselves and the knights."

Interrupting Beryl protested, "They are warriors! They will not listen to talks of peace!"

"Be silent! You have had your say. Please continue Carmine," offered the dragon leader.

She continued, "Representatives from each of the clans could arrange a meeting with the king and some of his knights to work out a plan for peace and unity."

"Thank you," said Brenthos. "We will now hear from Aurum."

The Golden dragon stood trembling before his fellow Kruppa members. "H-H-Highly honored B-Brenthos and council members, I think it would be safest for us to r-r-retreat deep into the mountain caves where we will be free from the kn-n-nights' persecution. When knights no longer hunt dragons, we could return to the o-open places."

"Your thoughts are appreciated," stated the Grand Dragon.

"Ora, we will now listen to your idea."

"Most excellent Brenthos and members of the esteemed Kruppa, I feel our best chance for survival would be to find a suitable land with few or no people and certainly no kings or knights. Once we find this place, we should all move there and make it our new home," concluded the Komodo leader.

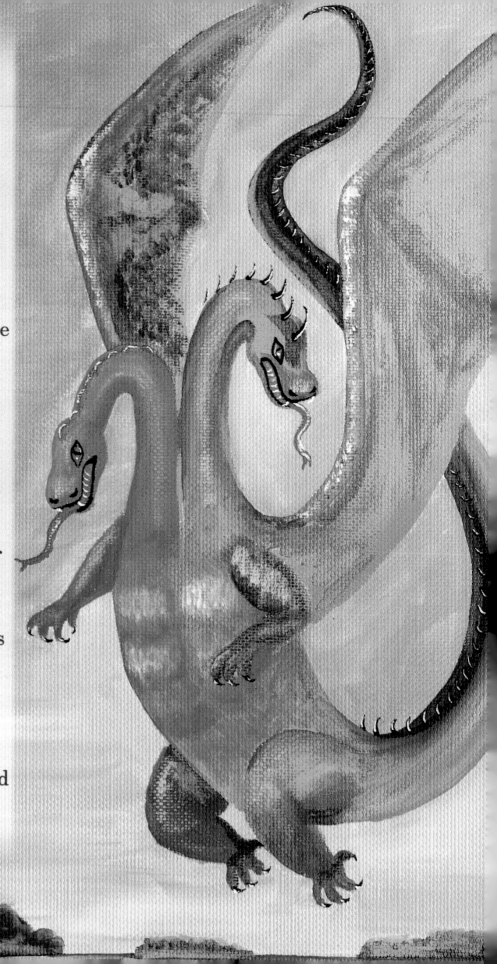

After careful consideration, the Grand Dragon announced he was most pleased with Ora's idea, and he ordered his two best scouts, Lokon and Pontis, to search for a suitable land where the dragons could relocate.

After many days the scouts returned, and they told of a place very far away completely surrounded by water with only a very few people, but plenty of deer, goats and boars for food. The Grand Dragon and the council decided that all dragons would leave their homes and move to this island.

Because of the danger on land, Brenthos decided it would be safest for the dragons to travel by way of the seas. This was simple for most dragons since most of them have wings. The only clan without wings, the Komodo Clan, is full of excellent swimmers, so they would swim below the flying dragons on the journey to their new home.

The dragons set off on their long journey under the light of a bright new moon, stopping only few times for food and rest. Lokon and Pontis continually flew ahead of the larger group keeping watch for the first sign of their new home and any trouble they might encounter.

One day as the sun was setting, the time finally came when the two scouts made a joyful announcement to the clans.

Lokon began, "Sisters and brothers, we have wonderful news."

Pontis continued, "We will reach our new home by the time the sun sinks into the ocean!" Then as one, the flying dragons raised their noble heads and breathed beautiful fire into the air as celebration. However, for a reason unknown to Brenthos and his troops, Ora and his clan failed to join them.

Shortly, the dragons reached their new home. The Komodo Clan crawled onto shore from the water, while the others landed gracefully from the air. Under the light of an even brighter and newer moon, Brenthos called together all the dragons and encouraged them to make the most of their new home. After addressing the large crowd, Brenthos held a private meeting with the Kruppa. Brenthos was concerned about Ora and the Komodo Clan because they hadn't joined in the fiery celebration.

Ora assured Brenthos that they too were greatly pleased at reaching their new home, but for some reason they were unable to breathe fire when they tried. Ora told the council his theory on the problem. "I believe our extremely long exposure to water has temporarily robbed us of our fire-breathing ability, but I am hopeful and confident it will return shortly."

As darkness fell on the tiny island, the dragons began a celebration which lasted for many days. The dragons sang songs, danced dances, told tales, and used their fiery breath to light up the dark skies at night. They also used the flames to entertain each other by creating fiery images in the air. The Emerald, Crimson and Golden Clans held competitions with each other to see who could hold their flame the longest or produce the brightest fire. During the celebration, the Komodo Clan served as judges for the flame competitions since their flame had not yet returned.

Using their flames so freely was a special treat for the dragons. While living in their old land, the dragons only used their fiery breath on rare occasions. If they used it often or in open places they would have been easily spotted by dragon-hunting knights. Now since there were no knights for the dragons to fear, they flamed very regularly. The dragons loved being able to breathe fire whenever they wanted, so they would flame often simply to admire the fire. Brenthos and the Kruppa decided to name their new home Flame Island, since they could now flame whenever they wanted.

The only bad thing the dragons noticed about flaming was the smoke that accompanied it. Each time a dragon flamed, smoke would be produced. The smoke caused the dragons to cough a little, and sometimes it burned their eyes. However, the dragons felt like those minor discomforts were worth it.

The dragons grew to love their new home very much. There was plenty of room and food for all the dragons. Since there was nothing for them to fear on the island, the dragons were free to roam, by land or air, anywhere they chose. The Kruppa would hold open meetings in front of all the dragons to discuss whatever was happening.

At one such meeting after the dragons had been on the island for several weeks, Ora addressed the crown. "Fellow dragons, it is with great regret that I inform you that I am now sure the flame of the Komodo Clan is lost forever."

This saddened all the clans, and Brenthos made a declaration. "From this day forward a month of flame-fasting will be held every year to remember the month long swim that cost the Komodo's their flame. The first Flame-fast will begin today."

After the month of flame-fasting was over, life returned to normal for the dragons. The flying dragons continued to flame very often, and they also began to cough even more often. Ora, who often served as doctor for the dragons, grew concerned with the coughing, but he too, like the rest of the dragons felt the annoyance of a cough was well worth the power to flame. Ora knew that he and his Komodo brothers and sisters would gladly suffer with a slight cough, if they could regain their ability to flame.

One day when visiting Carmine, the Crimson leader, Ora noticed a beautiful rock painting. "That painting was done by my youngest daughter Cherron when we first arrived on Flame Island," Carmine told Ora.

"It is a lovely work, you should be proud," he commented. Even though Ora did not say anything to Carmine, he noticed something very disturbing about the painting. The bright colors Cherron had used helped him realize the flying dragons all seemed to have become slightly paler in color. Ora had learned many years ago that a dragon losing its color was losing its life.

Ora thought many hours and days about what he had seen, and as he watched the flying dragons over the next few weeks he noticed they were becoming even paler. However when the time of flame-fasting came, Ora discovered that the dragons' color brightened slightly during the month. However, when the dragons began flaming again, they grew paler. It was then that Ora deduced that either the flame or the smoke from the flame was killing the dragons. Ora suspected it was the smoke since it caused the coughing. After careful study Ora learned that the smoke allowed a type of Karkata to enter the dragons' lungs. Once the Karkata was in the lungs, it would spread to other parts of the body slowing killing the dragon.

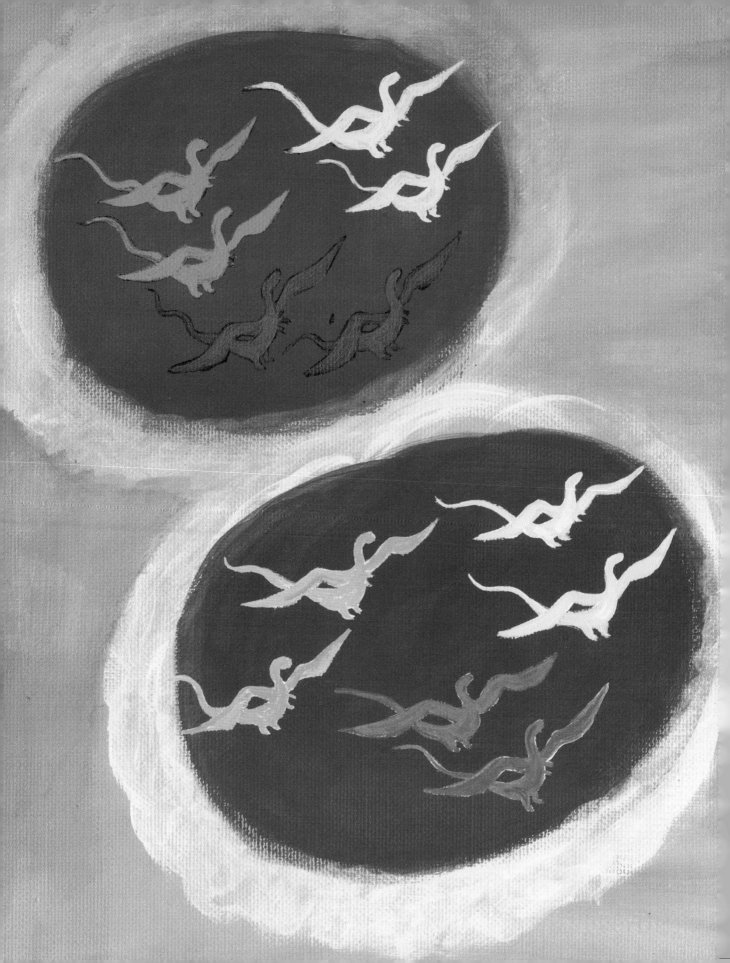

Ora told Brenthos of his discovery, and they called a special meeting of all the clans. "My children, Ora has given me some terrible and disturbing news. I know in my heart that what he is saying is true, so please listen to him and do exactly as he says," pleaded Brenthos.

"As I'm sure you've all noticed, the flying dragons are losing their colors. I'm sorry to say this means they are losing their lives as well. I have researched the problem and discovered that the smoke from flaming is causing this. The smoke has weakened the lungs and allowed a type of Karkata to enter them. Once the Karkata is in the lungs it spreads throughout the body. The only chance you have is to stop flaming, but it may already be too late. Since we, the Komodos, can no longer flame we seem to have escaped this terrible fate. I am truly sorry to bear such sad news."

Most of the dragons heeded their advice and stopped flaming, but others continued to flame even after the warning.

It wasn't very long after the meeting that dragons started to die. First those dragons that still flamed were gone, but soon after the flying dragons who had stopped after the warnings also began to die. They had not quit soon enough. In less than a year after Ora's discovery, all the fire-breathing-flying dragons were gone.

Ora and the Komodo Clan were the only one's who had survived. If they hadn't lost their flames on their long journey, there is no doubt that they would also be gone. After the deaths of their brothers and sisters, the Komodo Clan could no longer bear to call their home Flame Island, so they changed its name to Komodo Island.

If you travel to this island today, you can still find the clan there. Although if you do visit them, be careful because they are dragons, and they might mistake you for a knight.